by Jess Hernandez

illustrated by Mariano Epelbaum

CAPSTONE EDITIONS
a capstone imprint

First Day of Unicorn School is published by
Capstone Editions, an imprint of Capstone.
1710 Roe Crest Drive
North Mankato, Minnesota 56003
www.capstonepub.com

Library of Congress Cataloging-in-Publication Data is available on the Library of Congress website.

ISBN: 978-1-6844-6279-7 (hardcover)
ISBN: 978-1-6844-6796-9 (paperback)
ISBN: 978-1-6844-6326-8 (ebook PDF)

Summary: Milly is incredibly excited to go to Unicorn School, a school that accepts only the best and the brightest unicorns. There's only one problem: She isn't a unicorn! She's a donkey in a party hat. Milly first feels uncomfortable, but eventually she learns that she and the others at the school have more in common than she thought.

Designers: Lori Bye and Kay Fraser

Printed and bound in China. PO4971

For Ruyman,
who makes plungers look good.
–JH

To my little stars and their shiny
laughs that make me happy.
–ME

Milly squealed. After weeks of waiting, the letter finally arrived. Milly was officially accepted to Unicorn School.

She was thrilled. And completely terrified.

Unicorn School taught only the best and the brightest unicorns.

And that was Milly—if you ignored one tiny detail . . .

She wasn't a unicorn.

She was a donkey in a party hat.

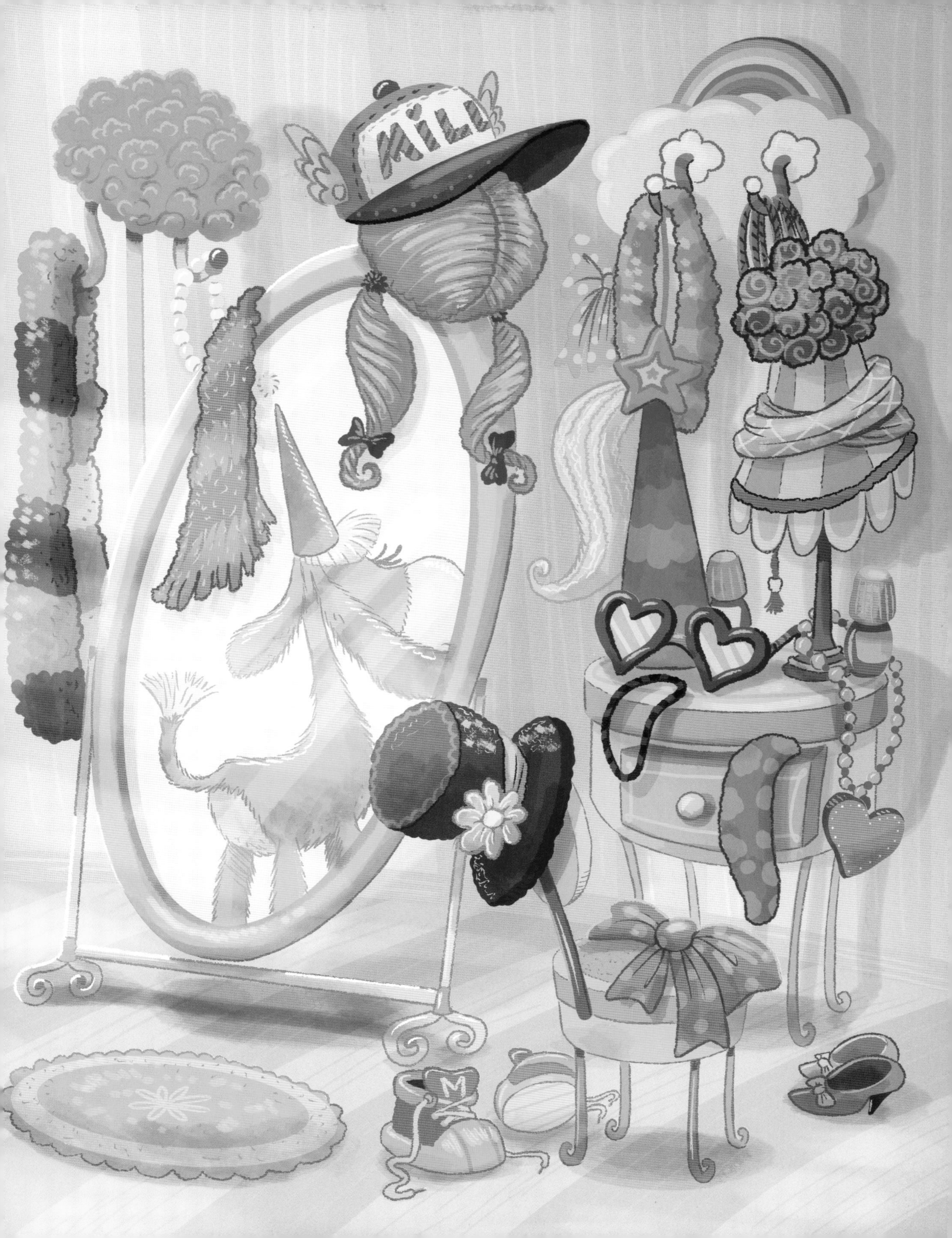
MiLL
M

So maybe she had sent a misleading picture—or two or three—with her application.

She considered not going. What if the other students noticed she didn't belong?

But then Milly pictured the school's sparkling fountains, lush gardens, and dragon-taming class. She had to go.

UNICORN SCHOOL

On her first day of school, Milly put on her hat,
fluffed her mane, and whispered, "I can do this!"
Then she trotted through the gate.

FIRST DAY OF UNICORN SCHOOL

UNICORN SCHOOL

The other unicorns all looked so well-groomed. Their hooves glittered like diamonds. Their manes shone in the sunlight. And their horns were polished and sparkly.

Milly was so distracted that she bumped right into a big unicorn with an extra sparkly horn.

"I'm sorry!" sputtered Milly.

"Mooo-ve it!" the unicorn cried. Then she gave her an odd look and stomped away.

Milly panicked. Was her horn crooked?

As she tried to check, she crashed into another unicorn. "Baaa-ck off!" he cried.

And another one. "Get off meeeh!" she bleated.

And another. "Not so ruff!" he barked.

One unicorn just spat.

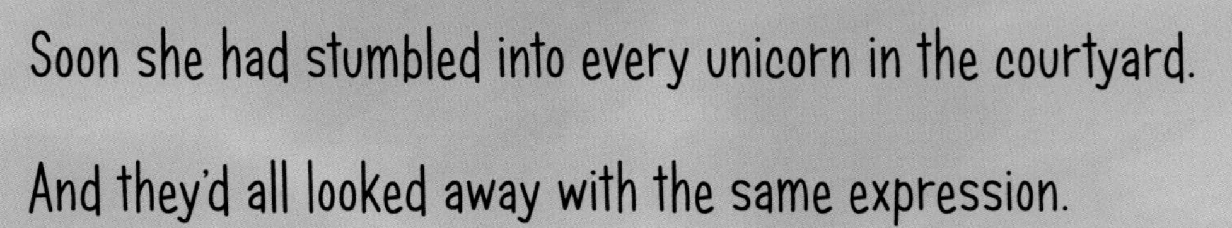

Soon she had stumbled into every unicorn in the courtyard.

And they'd all looked away with the same expression.

Milly's hat slid over one ear. Her eyes filled with tears.

She should have known this wouldn't work. She wasn't a unicorn. She was a donkey. And that's all she'd ever be.

She plodded toward the gate.

Milly turned around for one last look. But just before she opened the gate, she noticed something: EVERYONE'S horns were crooked!

"Hold it," said Milly.
"Are ANY of you
real unicorns?"

They baaed and hooted and mooed, but no one would speak. Finally—

"My horn's an ice cream cone,"
one horse confessed.

"Mine's a toilet plunger," said a goat in a wig.
"I painted it with nail polish."

"I glued sequins on a traffic cone," said
a cow, "and added hair extensions."

A zebra snickered. A sheep chuckled. Soon everyone was bleating, braying, and neighing with laughter.

Milly smiled. For the first time in her life, she fit right in.
THE AWESOME
ANIMAL SCHOOL
ALL ANIMALS ARE WELCOME!